Frog Power

Beverly Lewis

Beverly Lewis Books for Young Readers

PICTURE BOOK

Cows in the House

THE CUL-DE-SAC KIDS

The Double Dabble Surprise
The Chicken Pox Panic
The Crazy Christmas Angel Mystery
No Grown-ups Allowed
Frog Power
The Mystery of Case D. Luc
The Stinky Sneakers Mystery
Pickle Pizza
Mailbox Mania
The Mudhole Mystery
Fiddlesticks
The Crabby Cat Caper
Tarantula Toes
Green Gravy
Backyard Bandit Mystery
Tree House Trouble
The Creepy Sleep-Over
The Great TV Turn-Off
Piggy Party
The Granny Game
Mystery Mutt
Big Bad Beans

Katie and Jake and the Haircut Mistake

THE CUL-DE-SAC KIDS

Frog Power

— • —

Beverly Lewis

BETHANY HOUSE PUBLISHERS
MINNEAPOLIS, MINNESOTA 55438

Frog Power
Copyright © 1995
Beverly Lewis

Cover illustration by Paul Turnbaugh.
Story illustrations by Barbara Birch.

Published by Bethany House Publishers
A Ministry of Bethany Fellowship International
11400 Hampshire Avenue South
Minneapolis, Minnesota 55438
www.bethanyhouse.com

Printed in the United States of America by
Bethany Press International, Minneapolis, Minnesota 55438

Library of Congress Cataloging-in-Publication Data

Lewis, Beverly.
    Frog power / Beverly Lewis.
        p.   cm. — (The cul-de-sac kids ; 5)
    Summary: The inclusion of Jason's frog Croaker in the
Easter pet parade she is planning challenges Stacy's fear of
frogs.

    [1. Frogs—Fiction. 2. Pets—Fiction. 3. Fear—Fiction.
4. Easter—Fiction.] I. Title. II. Series: Lewis, Beverly.
Cul-de-sac kids ; 5.
PZ7.L58464Fr   1995
[Fic]—dc20   95–22385
ISBN 1–55661–645–7   CIP
                                       AC

To
Shanna Dreuth,
who likes slimy things.
Once she caught twelve frogs
and carried them in her pockets all day.

THE CUL-DE-SAC KIDS

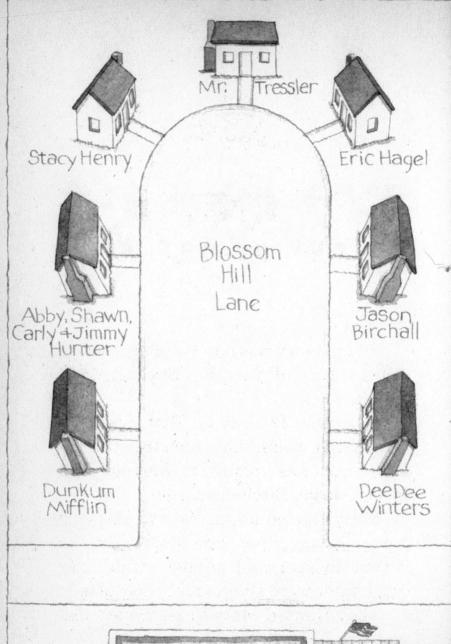

Mr. Tressler

Stacy Henry

Eric Hagel

Abby, Shawn, Carly & Jimmy Hunter

Jason Birchall

Blossom Hill Lane

Dunkum Mifflin

DeeDee Winters

Blossom Hill School

ONE

Stacy Henry was late for school. It was the first time all year. But Stacy couldn't help it.

Today was Pet Day for Miss Hershey's third-grade class. And something slimy and green was coming to Blossom Hill School. Jason Birchall said so.

Stacy tiptoed down the hall carrying her cockapoo puppy. She stopped at the classroom door and peeked inside. Her classmates were showing off their pets.

Abby Hunter, Stacy's best friend, was

cuddling Snow White, a fluffy white dog. Shawn Hunter, Abby's adopted Korean brother, was tickling Snow White's ears.

Stacy spotted Dunkum in the corner of the room. His real name was Edward Mifflin, but no one called him that. He was Dunkum, the tallest and the best basketball player in school.

Dunkum lifted Blinkee, his fat gray rabbit, out of the cage. He set her on his desk. Stepping back, he clapped his hands two times. Blinkee sat up on her haunches and wiggled her pink little nose. She was the cutest rabbit Stacy had ever seen.

Just then, a low croaking sound came from the middle of the classroom. Blinkee pricked up her long bunny ears.

Stacy shivered. She hid behind the classroom door. The croaking sound continued. *The slimy green nightmare is here! Jason Birchall's bullfrog is the worst creature God ever made,* she decided.

Stacy sneaked around the door and stared across the room. A glass aquarium sat on the desk behind hers. Inches from her desk was Jason's bullfrog. On top of its head, two eyes bulged out.

Stacy leaned against the classroom door, wishing she could go home. She put Sunday Funnies, her cockapoo, on the floor. He strained on his leash.

Abby and Shawn ran to Jason's desk to see the noisy bullfrog. Dunkum carried his rabbit over for a look. Soon, most of the class had gathered around the ten-gallon glass tank.

But not Stacy. She took a deep breath and crept to Miss Hershey's desk. Sunday Funnies followed on his leash.

The teacher smiled at her. "You're a little late today." She petted Sunday Funnies' head.

"I almost didn't come," Stacy blurted out.

Her teacher frowned. "I'm sorry to

hear that, Stacy. Are you feeling all right?"

"I'm not sick or anything." Stacy glanced over her shoulder. *Icksville! Why did Miss Hershey have to change the desks around yesterday?*

"Stacy? Is something wrong?" the teacher asked.

Stacy turned around slowly. "I, uh . . . no, I'm fine, thanks." Stacy inched toward her desk, past Eric Hagel.

Eric's hamster was nibbling on a piece of carrot inside his cage.

"Nice hamster," Stacy said. She hardly even looked at the hamster. Instead, she stared at Jason's bullfrog at the end of the row.

Eric coughed. "Earth to Stacy! Guess what I named my hamster?"

"I don't know," Stacy muttered. She was thinking about a slimy bullfrog named Croaker.

"Come on, just guess," Eric insisted.

"Uh . . . Slimy?" It was a dumb name for a hamster, but Stacy couldn't get the horrible green bullfrog off her mind.

"Not even close," Eric said.

"Then I give up," Stacy said flatly. The hamster made her sneeze.

"This is the smartest hamster in the world," Eric bragged. "Her name is Fran the Ham. And does she ever ham it up!" He laughed. "Get it—*ham* it up?"

"Of course I get it," Stacy snapped. And she clumped off to her desk wishing, wishing. She wished Jason Birchall would take Croaker home.

Shawn Hunter rushed over to Stacy's desk. He grinned. "I rub Sunday Funnies' neck, yes?"

Stacy nodded. "He likes you, Shawn. Ever since the day he got hit by a car and you helped him."

Shawn's eyes danced as he stroked the cockapoo.

Dunkum put his rabbit on the floor be-

13

side Sunday Funnies. The rabbit and the cockapoo sniffed each other. Sunday Funnies wagged his curly puff of a tail.

"I think they like each other," Dunkum said.

Stacy petted the rabbit. Her eyes began to water. She sneezed three times.

Miss Hershey asked everyone to sit down. "We have an exciting day ahead of us, class." She grinned. Everyone knew Miss Hershey loved animals.

Stacy grabbed a tissue from inside her desk and blew her nose. Then she put Sunday Funnies in her lap and cuddled him. "It's a good thing *you* don't make me sneeze," she whispered to him.

Suddenly, Jason Birchall reached over his desk. He was petting Sunday Funnies' head.

Stacy pulled her puppy away.

Jason frowned. "What's the matter with you?"

"Stay away from him," Stacy said.

14

Gently, she put her puppy on the floor and sat down. She slid her chair close to her desk. Far away from Jason's creepy bullfrog.

Her stomach was squished against the desk. But it was better than having frog breath in her hair!

TWO

Miss Hershey called roll. Then the kids began to show off their pets.

Eric Hagel lugged his hamster cage to the front of the room. *Kerplop!* He set it down on Miss Hershey's desk. "Meet my hamster, Fran the Ham."

The class giggled.

Eric continued. "Fran likes parade music." He grinned. "She likes 'Stars and Stripes Forever.'"

Miss Hershey sat at her desk. She leaned on her elbows, peering into the

hamster cage. "Does Fran do any tricks?" she asked.

Eric put his hands on his hips. "How many want to see Fran do her amazing routine?"

Everyone cheered.

"First, I have to get my tape recorder ready."

Jason groaned.

Turning around, Stacy muttered, "What's the matter? Isn't *Croaker* smart enough to do tricks?"

Jason shot her his best cross-eyes.

"Frog eyes," Stacy whispered.

Jason made another face.

Just then, the beat of drums filled the room. Brassy trumpets and trombones joined in.

Stacy couldn't believe it. Fran the Ham was running on a little turnwheel. Faster and faster! Fran's tiny hamster feet were flying.

"Now check this out," Eric told the

class. He pushed the stop button on the tape recorder.

Fran the Ham slowed down. She stopped!

The kids clapped with delight. Eric carried the hamster cage back to his seat.

Stacy pulled out a pencil and wrote a note.

Dear Eric,
    I really do like your hamster. She is very smart. I'm sorry I didn't believe you.
                    Your friend,
                    Stacy Henry

Stacy folded the note. She felt good about it. Eric was her neighbor on Blossom Hill Lane—their cul-de-sac. *And the Cul-de-sac Kids stick together, no matter what,* she remembered. That's the way it was.

Stacy stuck the note in her jeans

pocket. She would give the note to Eric at recess.

Miss Hershey called Shawn Hunter next.

Abby raised her hand. "Shawn and I want to show our dog together. Is that OK?"

Miss Hershey nodded.

Shawn led Snow White to the front of the room.

Abby followed, carrying a bag of doggie treats. "Shawn will introduce our dog," she said.

Shawn's dark eyes shone. "Snow White is shee-zoo puppy," he said. "Her family go back very long time—to Chinese courts. Long ago this kind of dog was watchdog."

Abby took off Snow White's leash. "Now Snow White will do some tricks for you," she announced.

Abby moved her arm in circles without saying a word. Snow White rolled over three times. Abby gave her a treat. Snow White chomped it right down.

Next Snow White played dead. The class called out her name. Jason hopped out of his seat and tickled Snow White's ear. The dog didn't budge an inch!

At last, Shawn snapped his fingers. Snow White leaped up for another treat.

The kids clapped loudly.

Abby and Shawn took their seats. Snow White sat on the floor near Shawn's desk.

Miss Hershey checked her record book. "Jason Birchall, you're next."

When Jason stood up, Stacy scooted down in her seat. Far away from the bullfrog behind her.

The glass cage was too heavy to move. So Jason was going to show off Croaker from his desk.

Stacy peeked around her chair.

Whoosh! Jason took off the wood frame. A silly grin stretched across his face. Then he reached inside.

Stacy shivered as Jason's hands caught the slimy green bullfrog.

Icksville! She covered her eyes.

THREE

Jason held his frog high. "This is Croaker." He pointed to the round spots behind the frog's eyes. "These are Croaker's ears. He can hear sounds under water."

Jason pranced around his desk. Even with his medicine, he was still hyper sometimes. Up and down the row he paced, showing off his bullfrog.

Some of the kids were brave. They touched Croaker's skin. When Jason stopped at Abby Hunter's desk, she stuck her pointer finger out. Then she closed her eyes, wrinkled her nose, and touched him. Her eyes popped open. "Ew!"

Jason skipped up to Stacy's desk. "It's *your* turn." He held the frog in front of her face.

What's it feel like? Stacy wondered. She stared at the frog. "I pass," she said, sliding back in her seat.

Jason grinned. "You sure?"

"Uh-huh." Stacy looked into the giant eyes of the bullfrog. She felt sick.

Quick as a flash, Croaker leaped out of Jason's hands . . . and into Stacy's lap!

"Get it off me!" she screamed. Her fingers bumped against the bullfrog's skin. "Ick!"

Before Jason could grab him, Croaker jumped off Stacy's lap and landed on Dunkum's desk.

"I catch! I catch!" Shawn cried in broken English. Letting go of Snow White's leash, Shawn dashed after Croaker. Then

Snow White darted after Shawn, barking loudly.

Soon . . . .

Sunday Funnies was yipping.

Fran the Ham was twittering.

Croaker was croaking.

Cats were meowing.

A parrot was screeching.

But Miss Hershey was silent. She simply sat at her desk and smiled.

After chasing the frog around the room two more times, Jason caught Croaker. He put him back in the cage and closed the wooden lid. "There," said Jason. "I think he needs my hyper medicine."

Eric laughed. So did the other boys.

Stacy didn't think it was funny. She raised her hand. "May I be excused, please?"

Miss Hershey nodded.

Stacy dashed out of the classroom and down the hall. It was time to get rid of the froggy feel on her hands.

27

The girls' room was empty. *Good,* she thought. Filling her hands with liquid soap, Stacy scrubbed and rubbed and scrubbed some more.

Suddenly, Stacy heard a strange sound. It was coming from the stall behind her. She listened. *What on earth?* She dried her hands and waited.

There it was again. It sounded like . . .

Out from under the door scampered her puppy.

"Sunday Funnies!" she cried. "*What* are you doing?"

The puppy's head was dripping wet.

"Oh, you're thirsty, is that it?" Stacy shook her finger at him. "Toilets are not for drinking." And she went into the stall to check.

Thank goodness, the toilet was flushed! Stacy lathered up her hands with soap and washed Sunday Funnies' head and face.

Then she held him up to the dryer.

28

Minutes later, Miss Hershey came in. "Are you all right, Stacy?"

Stacy nodded. "Everything's under control . . . now."

Miss Hershey touched Stacy's shoulder. "Let's get you back to class. I think you'll like the story today."

Stacy followed Miss Hershey down the hall. She wanted to forget about Jason's bullfrog. Forever.

"We're reading 'The Frog Prince,'" Miss Hershey said as she opened the classroom door.

Stacy dragged her feet. She felt worse than ever. It was bad enough having a frog breathe down her neck. Now she had to read about one, too!

"Super icksville," she muttered on the way to her desk. *Who wants to read THAT fairy tale?*

She looked at the clock. Fifteen minutes till recess. Fifteen minutes too many!

FOUR

"Once upon a time . . ."

Stacy heard the class reading out loud. She skipped ahead to the pictures. An ugly green frog was in a well and a princess was crying. She remembered the beginning of the story.

"What's wrong, little Princess?" the frog asked.

The princess sobbed. "My beautiful gold necklace has fallen into the well."

"Dry your tears," croaked the frog. "I can help. What will you give me if I find it?"

"Whatever you wish, my dear frog," said the princess.

Stacy wanted to choke. Who ever heard of calling a frog *my dear*?

Finding her place, Stacy continued to read. The frog was doing a good job of tricking the princess. He wanted to have supper with her and drink from her silver cup!

The princess wiped her tears and nodded yes.

"And that's not all I want," the frog said.

The princess looked surprised. "What else?"

"I want to sleep in your fine house."

She looked at the frog. "I know just the place for you. Will you get my golden necklace now?" the princess begged.

"One more thing." The frog's eyes blinked.

"I want to be friends."

Stacy slammed the book shut. This was too much!

A low croaking sound made her jump. Jason's bullfrog was at it again.

Stacy spun around. "Keep your frog quiet!" she whispered.

Jason frowned. "He's hungry. Wanna help me catch bugs at recess?"

Bugs!
Bullfrogs!
Frog fairy tales!
What a horrible day!

Stacy watched the second hand on the clock. 5. . . . 4. . . . 3. . . . 2. . . . 1. . . . Recess!

The bell rang and Stacy was the first one outside. She walked Sunday Funnies around the playground on his leash.

Jason and Eric were digging for ants near the sidewalk. Probably to feed that dumb old frog. Stacy handed Eric the note she'd written. Then she ran to the swings.

Soon, Abby and her little sister Carly came over. Carly was in first grade. She held the leashes for Snow White and Sunday Funnies while the girls swang.

Abby leaned back, pulling hard against the swing. "Do you like 'The Frog Prince' so far?"

"It's OK, I guess," Stacy said.

Abby smiled. "I like the ending best."

"I haven't read the ending yet," Stacy said.

"Why not?" Abby asked.

Stacy shook her head. "It gives me the creeps. My dad was reading the story to me the day he left me and my mom."

Abby twisted her swing and let it spin.

Stacy copied her friend and whirled around. She could almost hear her dad's voice reading out loud to her. She pushed her sneakers against the sand.

Abby changed the subject. "Let's dye Easter eggs at my house next week."

Stacy didn't want to think about Easter eggs. Another holiday without her dad.

Stacy jumped out of the swing. "I know! Let's do something different this year."

"Like what?" Abby asked. She held the leashes for Snow White and Sunday Funnies so Carly could swing.

"Let's have an Easter pet parade," Stacy shouted.

"Double dabble good idea," Abby said.

"Goody!" Carly said. Her golden curls shone in the sunlight.

"Count the pets in the cul-de-sac," Stacy said.

"Let's see. There's Snow White and Sunday Funnies," said Abby.

"Don't forget our baby ducks, Quacker and Jack," Carly said, swinging higher. "One belongs to Jimmy and one is mine." Jimmy was the younger of Abby and Carly's two Korean brothers.

Abby pulled a tablet and pen out of her

jeans pocket. "There's Blinkee, Dunkum's rabbit, and Dee Dee's cat, Mister Whiskers. That makes six."

"And Eric's hamster, Fran the Ham," said Stacy. "That's seven."

"Er-rib-bit!" Carly stopped the swing with her feet. "Don't forget Jason's bullfrog." She giggled and ran to catch up with her friend Dee Dee.

Stacy shivered. No way did she want Croaker in *her* pet parade!

The recess bell rang. "Since we only have a half day today, let's have a meeting after school," Abby said.

"Good idea," Stacy said. And she ran across the playground, with her puppy scampering ahead.

The line for Miss Hershey's class was full of kids with pets. Sunday Funnies barked at Jason. Croaker was sitting inside Jason's shirt pocket! Bulging eyes stuck out over the top of his pocket.

Abby laughed. "What's Croaker doing out here?"

"Frogs need exercise, too," Jason explained.

Eric turned around. "Animals need attention, whether they're ugly or not."

Shawn laughed a high-pitched giggle.

Stacy didn't feel like laughing at all.

FIVE

Stacy was glad school was out early. She went with Abby to pick up Carly after school. Carly was waiting with Dee Dee Winters beside the first-grade door.

Shawn and Jimmy, Abby's Korean brothers, walked with them across the playground.

Jason's mom picked him up in her car. The frog aquarium was too heavy to carry home.

Soon, Eric came with Fran the Ham, and Dunkum with Blinkee. The Cul-de-sac Kids always walked together. It was one of Abby's ideas. She was the president of the Cul-de-sac Kids—nine kids who lived on Blossom Hill Lane.

Carly and Dee Dee held hands as they skipped. Stacy remembered holding hands with Abby when they were in first grade. That had been the year after Stacy's dad moved out.

"Spring is almost here!" Abby shouted.

The sun was warm on Stacy's back. "And then comes summer!" she squealed.

"Yes! School over in two months," Shawn yelled.

Dunkum and Eric had their hands full with cages. One for Blinkee and one for Fran the Ham. Shawn helped Eric carry his tape recorder.

Just then, Abby turned around in the middle of the cul-de-sac. "Everyone meet at Dunkum's after lunch," she said. "We have important things to discuss."

Carly giggled. "I already know what Abby's gonna say."

"What is meeting about?" little Jimmy asked.

"Come and find out," Dee Dee bossed.

"Abby, you tell now!" Jimmy yelled.

"It's not really a secret," Abby told her brother and all the kids. "But we could surprise our parents for Easter."

"Yes, let's," said Stacy. She couldn't wait for the meeting.

"What surprise?" Jimmy asked.

"Stacy is planning a pet parade," said Abby.

The kids liked the idea. Stacy could tell by the way everyone hurried home for lunch.

She unlocked her front door and went to fix a sandwich. "It's just you and me," she said to Sunday Funnies. She poured dog food into his dish. Standing up, she saw a note stuck to the refrigerator. "What's this?"

Stacy began to read.

Dear Stacy,
     Your father called this morning.
He's going to be in town over Easter
and wants to see us. We'll talk to-
night, OK?

                    Love you, honey—
                    Mom

"Listen to this!" Stacy sat down beside her puppy and read the note out loud. She hugged Sunday Funnies. It was a strange name for a dog, but it fit. He could sniff out the Sunday newspaper and find the funny papers. Before anyone else!

A tall paper hat—made from the Sunday comics—would be the perfect Easter hat for him. Stacy could almost see the cul-de-sac pets marching, hopping, and jumping down Blossom Hill Lane. The pet parade would be the perfect Easter surprise for her dad!

Stacy made a peanut butter and jelly

sandwich. She drank a glass of milk with it. Nibbling on an apple, Stacy dashed off to Dunkum's.

She passed Jason Birchall's house on the way. Just thinking about Croaker made her shiver. He was the ugliest creature on earth.

Stacy wished Jason's bullfrog would go jump in a well. Then the pet parade would be perfect!

SIX

Stacy tossed her sneakers beside the steps in Dunkum's basement. Sitting on the floor, she finished eating her apple.

Dunkum whistled and the kids got quiet.

Abby plopped down in her president's seat—the blue beanbag. "OK," she began. "Is everyone here?"

The kids looked around.

"Someone's missing," Abby said.

Eric pushed his hair back. "Did we forget to tell Jason?"

"I thought *you* told him," Dunkum said.

Shawn stood up. "I go get Jason."

Stacy felt funny inside.

When Shawn came back with Jason, the Cul-de-sac Kids began to plan the parade.

"Stacy is a good fixer-upper," Abby said. "She should be in charge of arranging the pets."

Dunkum brought a marker board from his father's study. He handed a blue marker to Stacy. "You make a list of all the girl animals." He drew a black line dividing the board in half. "I'll write the boy animals on this side."

Girls	Boys
Quacker—	Jack—
Carly's duck	Jimmy's duck
Snow White—	Mr. Whiskers—
Shawn's dog	Dee Dee's cat

46

Blinkee—	Sunday Funnies—
Dunkum's	Stacy's dog
rabbit	
Fran the Ham—	Croaker—
Eric's hamster	Jason's bullfrog

Stacy turned around. "What about *you*, Abby?"

Shawn leaped off the floor. "Abby play march tape on tape recorder."

"Good idea!" Stacy said.

"Or, Abby could pull a wagon full of my grandpa's birdcages. He has three canaries and two parakeets," Eric suggested.

Stacy looked at Abby. "Wanna?"

Abby nodded. "I'll carry the tape recorder in one hand, and pull the wagon with the other."

"I could buy a *lady* frog for you," Jason said. "Would you like that?"

"Uh . . . that's OK," Stacy said quickly. "Abby is our props manager and bird tamer. Besides, one frog on the block is enough."

47

Carly and Dee Dee giggled.

"Let's make Easter bonnets for the girl animals," said Stacy. "Who wants to help me make them?"

Abby shot up her hand.

"What about bow ties for the boy animals?" Eric said. "Hey, Stacy, wanna help me?"

Stacy smiled. "OK!"

"Good idea," Jason croaked. "I'll help, too. Er-rib-bit!"

Stacy groaned. Had Eric tricked her into touching Croaker? Again?

Abby ended the meeting. "Remember, don't tell your parents. It's a big surprise. Stacy's head of the parade. She'll make sure all the animals are dressed for the show."

Stacy scrambled for her sneakers. Keeping a secret was not a problem. But tying a bow around a bullfrog's neck? *That* was a problem!

SEVEN

Stacy ran home to clean her room. Something bugged her about Jason's horrible frog. What was it?

She stood on a chair and dusted the shelf in her closet. In the back, Stacy found her old fairy-tale book.

She jumped off the chair and sat on her bed. Slowly, she turned the pages. It was filled with beautiful pictures. And memories of her dad.

Stacy picked up the bookmark. It had marked the spot in the middle of the story.

The one her father was reading to her before he left.

Stacy turned the page. "Oh no!" Staring up from the page was a giant green bullfrog. The story was "The Frog Prince"—the same one that Stacy was reading for school.

Whoosh! Stacy slammed the book shut. A puff of dust flew out. "I hate this story!" she yelled. "I hate frogs!"

Stacy stomped out of her bedroom and down the hall. It was time to think about Easter bonnets and bow ties. Anything but frogs!

In the living room, Stacy searched through old newspapers. She found the Sunday paper from last week.

Her puppy scampered down the hall. He nosed his way into the comics. He'd found them again!

Stacy held up the color page to her face and sniffed. It didn't smell any different from the other pages. She snuggled her puppy. "How do you do it, you silly?"

Stacy folded the comics page in half and began to make a tall pointed hat. She found scissors and glue in the kitchen. Then she made a bow tie to match.

Stacy giggled as she dressed Sunday Funnies. She picked him up and ran to her room. Standing in front of the long mirror, she held her puppy up. "You'll be the star of the Easter parade."

"Woof!" Sunday Funnies agreed.

Stacy heard the garage door rumble. "Mom's home!" She hid the Easter hat and bow tie in her closet. Then she ran to the top of the steps. She couldn't wait to find out more about her dad. Was he *really* coming?

Her mother hugged her close when she came in. "Hi, honey, how was school?"

"OK." She followed her mother into the kitchen.

Her mother sat at the kitchen table. "Whew! I need a vacation."

"Disneyland?" Stacy suggested.

Stacy's mother chuckled. "That's not what I had in mind." She went to the refrigerator. When she opened the door, the note fell off.

Stacy ran to pick up the note. Now was her big chance. "Why is Daddy coming to town?"

"He's coming on business and . . ." Stacy's mother stopped for a second. "He wants to see you."

Stacy held up the note. "This says he wants to see *us*." Stacy hoped that meant something. Maybe Daddy was coming back!

"He's coming Friday afternoon," her mother said.

Three days from now! "Let's invite him for supper," Stacy pleaded.

"Not this time," her mother said.

Stacy left the room. "Not this time," she whispered to herself. "Not this time and not ever!" Why couldn't her parents at least be friends?

Stacy went to her room and closed the door. She found her storybook. It reminded her of the best days of her life.

"Let's find out what happens to the frog prince," she said to Sunday Funnies.

Happy and sad feelings jumbled up inside her. She found the bookmark and began to read.

EIGHT

Stacy pretended her father was sitting next to her. Reading out loud to her.

The princess was talking to the frog. "I promise to do everything you said." But the princess secretly hoped the frog would forget. She didn't want a nasty frog coming into the castle! But she said it again, "I promise."

The frog went down, down. Deep into the well. The princess watched and waited.

Up he came with the gold necklace in

his mouth. He tossed it onto the grass.

"Oh!" said the princess. "My beautiful necklace!" And she picked it up and ran away.

"Wait a minute!" croaked the frog. "You forgot to take me with you."

But the princess didn't wait for the frog. She ran all the way to the castle. And soon she forgot about him.

Stacy stopped reading. *What a horrible girl,* she thought. *The princess didn't even say thank you.*

Stacy stared at the picture of the princess.

Knockity-knock!

Stacy jumped. "Come in."

It was Abby. She was carrying a white plastic bag. "Hi, Stacy. What are you doing?"

"Reading." Stacy showed the book to her friend.

"Oh, I like the bright colors," Abby said. "Where'd you get it?"

"From my dad." Stacy turned to the front of the book. "It was a birthday present a long time ago."

Abby smiled. "It's really nice."

Stacy moved over on the bed. "Guess what?"

"You hate Jason's bullfrog, right?"

Stacy felt uneasy. "It's just so . . . uh, so ugly."

"God made lots of weird-looking animals," Abby said. "And my dad thinks God probably laughs about it sometimes."

Stacy nodded. Abby was lucky to have a father who loved God—even though it wasn't luck at all.

"My dad's coming for a visit this Friday," Stacy said.

"Double dabble good!" Abby said. "What a fantastic Good Friday present."

"I hope so." Stacy felt the sad and happy feelings again.

NINE

"I haven't seen my dad in a long time," Stacy said. "It's a little scary."

"You'll do OK," Abby said softly. "You love your dad, right?"

Stacy sat up straight. "I'm worried that Mom might get mad."

Abby leaned closer. "Why would she?"

"If I'm nice to my dad, my mom might get upset." Stacy hugged the storybook.

Abby touched Stacy's hand. "Just be yourself. I like you best that way."

"It's not easy sometimes," Stacy replied. "Not around my parents."

Abby raised her eyebrows. "Why not?"

"Because I don't want to hurt either one of them. Your parents aren't divorced. Maybe you don't understand."

Abby nodded. "You're right. I can't imagine my dad not living with us."

Stacy grabbed Abby's hand. She felt tears slide down her cheek.

Abby bowed her head. "Let's pray, OK?" Abby was like that. She prayed anytime. Anywhere.

"Dear Lord," she began. "I don't understand about divorce, but you do. Help Stacy have a good time with her father when he comes." Abby took a deep breath. "And help Stacy remember that Jason's bullfrog is part of your creation. In Jesus' name, Amen."

"Amen," Stacy repeated. She felt warm all over.

Abby pulled some tissue paper out of her plastic bag. "Carly and I made hat patterns for all the pets." She held up some tissue paper. Some were little. Some big.

"How cute," Stacy said. "But can a rabbit wear a hat?"

Abby giggled. She wiggled her fingers. "Right between his ears," she said.

Stacy went to the closet. She found Sunday Funnies' bow tie. "Look what I made."

"Hey, you're good," Abby exclaimed. "Let's make everything out of the Sunday comics."

"How about a hat-fitting party tomorrow after school?" Stacy suggested. "For girl animals only."

"Double dabble good!" Abby said.

"Let's meet at the end of the cul-de-sac," Stacy said. "Between Mr. Tressler's house and the old oak tree." She followed Abby to the front door.

"It's the perfect place," Abby said as she left.

Stacy couldn't wait.

TEN

After school, Stacy measured the girl pets for their tall Easter bonnets. "Ah-choo!" She couldn't stop sneezing. Pet allergies were no fun!

Blinkee twitched her long bunny ears as Stacy tried to measure around them. Abby held Blinkee still.

Next came Fran the Ham. Eric bribed her with a carrot while Stacy measured. Now Stacy's eyes were itchy. Super itchy!

"Ah-choo!" Stacy blew her nose. "This is horrible," she said.

"Here." Abby gave her a clean tissue. "Cover your nose with this."

"And try not to breathe," teased Eric.

Quacker and Snow White were last. The tissue didn't help. Stacy's eyes watered even more.

She thought about the Easter parade—a good surprise for her father. For *all* the parents in the cul-de-sac. No way would she give up! Not even for allergies!

After supper, Stacy made herself a mask from an old T-shirt. She cut holes for the eyes. *This will keep me from sneezing,* she thought. Then she headed to Dee Dee's house.

Dee Dee giggled when she saw the mask.

Stacy measured Mister Whisker's neck. "Bow ties look cool on cats," she teased.

Then Stacy hurried to Abby's house to measure Jimmy's duck, Jack. Dunkum and Eric came along to help.

"Bow ties look so classy on a duck," Abby said.

Jimmy held the duck's fluffy body still. Dunkum wrote down the inches on some paper.

"Simply ducky," Eric said, laughing.

Stacy smiled through the mask. She stood up to leave. Glancing across the street, she thought about Jason's slimy bullfrog. She shivered. *Icksville!*

"You won't need your mask at Jason's," Abby said.

"Why not?" Stacy asked.

Eric cackled. "Frogs can't make you sneeze."

"Hey, do you know what a frog uses to cook supper?" Dunkum joked.

Jimmy shook his head. "Frog cannot cook."

"It's just a joke," Abby told her little brother.

"What *does* a frog cook supper in?" asked Stacy.

66

"A croakpot, of course!" Dunkum said, pretending to shoot a basket.

The kids giggled.

Stacy said, "Good joke, but now I've got work to do. Alone." And she wandered across the street. She held her breath inside her mask as she went.

Jason answered the door. "What's the mask for?"

"Some animals bug me," Stacy said. "I'm itchy and sneezy."

"Croaker won't bother you," Jason said.

That's what you think, thought Stacy. "So, what's your frog's neck size?" she asked.

Jason took the lid off the aquarium. "How should I know?"

Stacy stepped back. "Uh, don't take him out yet."

"Why not?"

"Because I don't like frogs," Stacy blurted.

Jason pushed up his glasses. "You don't?"

Stacy sat down. "I'm sorry, Jason. It's not your fault."

"That's OK. Frogs aren't for everyone."

Stacy nodded. "I guess that's why God made dogs and cats and ducks."

"Here, I'll measure Croaker's neck for you." Jason took the yellow measuring tape from Stacy.

She watched Jason touch his frog. She thought about the frog in her storybook. She tried to imagine Croaker making a deal with a real live princess.

Stacy stopped sneezing and took off her mask. Slowly, she inched closer to the green bullfrog. "Jason?"

"Yeah?"

"Will Croaker jump down the street in our parade?"

"You betcha! All you need is a fly on the end of a string," Jason said.

"He won't jump away and get lost?" Stacy asked.

"Don't worry," Jason said. "I'll catch him if he does."

Stacy carried her T-shirt mask home. She couldn't wait to find out what happened at the end of "The Frog Prince."

Maybe frogs weren't so bad after all.

ELEVEN

Stacy ran to her room and began to read.

The frog was sad because the princess had not kept her promise.

One day, there was a slippery knock on the castle door. A hoarse voice called, "Princess, princess, open up! Let me sip from your golden cup!"

The princess ran to the door and looked out. When she saw the frog, she almost slammed the door. But there was a tear on the frog's face.

"Why are you crying?" asked the princess.

"I am lonely," he said. "I want to be your friend."

The princess began to cry, too. She was as lonely as the green frog. "Come in. We will have tea." And she wiped her eyes and bent down to pick up the frog.

But when she did, the frog disappeared! In its place stood a tall prince with gentle brown eyes. And he was smiling at her.

"Oh, thank you, dear Princess!" The prince tipped his hat. "Your kindness did the trick at last."

The princess began to dance and sing. The prince took her hand, and they danced and sang together.

★　★　★

Then the doorbell rang and Stacy hurried to meet Abby. "You were right," Stacy said. "The ending is great!"

Abby sat on the floor. "It's not just a good ending, it's a good beginning, too!"

Stacy understood. In fairy tales, people live happily ever after. In real life, it's not that easy.

"It's just a story," Abby reminded Stacy. "Let's make the parade outfits."

"OK." But Stacy opened the storybook to the last page. One more time.

A round, gold coach with six white horses drove up to the castle. The frog prince whisked the princess off to the royal wedding.

Stacy sighed. "My family needs some frog power."

Abby smiled. She traced the hat patterns on tissue paper. "Your parents are talking to each other. *That's* a good sign. Maybe someday they'll be friends."

Stacy sat beside Abby and cut out the bonnets. With all her heart, she hoped Abby was right.

Just then Stacy's mom knocked on the

door. Quickly, the girls hid the parade stuff under the bed.

"Come in!" Stacy called when it was all clear.

Her mother carried a tray of cookies. "Hungry, girls?"

"Thanks," Abby said.

"Oh, this reminds me," Stacy said, taking a cookie. "I need some flies to feed Jason's bullfrog."

Stacy's mother raised her eyebrows. "Flies?"

"Frogs get hungry, too," Stacy explained.

"You could ask your father about it when he comes for supper tomorrow," said her mother.

Stacy couldn't help herself. She shouted, "Thank you! Oh, Mommy, thank you!"

Of course, it wasn't gold coaches or white horses. And it certainly wasn't

promises or gold necklaces. But it was *something*.

Something very special.

THE CUL-DE-SAC KIDS SERIES
Don't miss #6!

THE MYSTERY OF CASE D. LUC

Dunkum's new basketball has been signed by his hero, David Robinson. Now Dunkum spends all his free time playing with the ball. And not his Cul-de-sac friends.

When the ball disappears, Dunkum finds a secret code. Someone with a strange name has stolen the basketball! And he is leaving codes everywhere!

Who *is* the mysterious Case D. Luc? And will the codes lead Dunkum to his basketball?

Also by Beverly Lewis

GIRLS ONLY (GO!)
Youth Fiction

Dreams on Ice   A Perfect Match
Only the Best   Reach for the Stars
Follow the Dream

SUMMERHILL SECRETS
Youth Fiction

Whispers Down the Lane   House of Secrets
Secret in the Willows   Echoes in the Wind
Catch a Falling Star   Hide Behind the Moon
Night of the Fireflies   Windows on the Hill
A Cry in the Dark   Shadows Beyond the Gate

HOLLY'S HEART SERIES
Youth Fiction

Holly's First Love   Straight-A Teacher
Secret Summer Dreams   The "No-Guys" Pact
Sealed With a Kiss   Little White Lies
The Trouble With Weddings   Freshmen Frenzy
California Christmas   Mystery Letters
Second-Best Friend   Eight Is Enough
Good-bye, Dressel Hills   It's a Girl Thing

THE HERITAGE OF LANCASTER COUNTY
Adult Fiction

The Shunning   The Confession
The Reckoning

OTHER ADULT FICTION

The Postcard   The Crossroad

The Sunroom

ABOUT THE AUTHOR

Beverly Lewis grew up in Pennsylvania with lots of pets. Maxie was the family's Eskimo Spitz. Trixie was their sad-eyed cocker spaniel. Goldie and Angie were the cats. Earl was the canary who hated violin music. And there was a giant box turtle, too, but never a frog.

Other books featuring pets by Beverly are:

The Six-Hour Mystery and sequel, *Mystery at Midnight*. And *all* the books in the Cul-De-Sac Kids series!